cH

The
Vampire
Bunny

The Vampire Bunny

by **James Howe**

Illustrated by **Jeff Mack**

Atheneum Books for Young Readers
New York   London   Toronto   Sydney   Singapore

Atheneum Books for Young Readers

An imprint of Simon & Schuster Children's Publishing Division

1230 Avenue of the Americas, New York, New York 10020

Text adapted by Heather Henson from *Bunnicula: A Rabbit-tale of Mystery* by Deborah and James Howe

Book design by Abelardo Martínez

The text for this book is set in Century Old Style.

The illustrations for this book are rendered in acrylic.

Printed in the United States of America

First Edition

10 9 8 7 6 5 4 3 2 1

CIP data for this book is available from the Library of Congress.

ISBN 0-689-85724-1

In memory of Deborah Howe
—J. H.

Many thanks to Steve Cerio
—J. M.

CHAPTER 1:

The Arrival

My name is Harold. I am a dog. I live with the Monroes: Toby and Pete and Mr. and Mrs. Monroe.

Chester lives here, too. Chester is a cat, but I like him anyway.

Things were pretty normal until Bunnicula arrived. Bunnicula came to us one dark and stormy night. It happened like this.

The Monroes were going to the movies.

"Take care of the house, Harold," they said. "You're the watchdog." That's what they always say when they go out.

On this evening the wind was howling. Lightning was flashing. Rain was falling. I thought it was a good night to be inside. The Monroes must have thought so, too. Suddenly they burst through the door.

"He's mine, I found him!" Toby yelled.

"You sat on him, you mean!" Pete yelled back.

"I found him," Toby repeated. "And he's sleeping in my room."

My ears perked up. I often sleep in Toby's room. On Fridays, Toby has late-night snacks. My favorite is chocolate cupcakes with cream in the middle. But that's another story.

In this story Mr. Monroe said, "Stop fighting, you two. The rabbit stays right here in the living room."

Rabbit?

Chester and I looked at each other. And then we took a closer look at what Mr. Monroe was holding. It was a shoe box. But inside the shoe box was a tiny black and white creature. It had long ears and a puff of a tail.

So this is a rabbit, I thought.

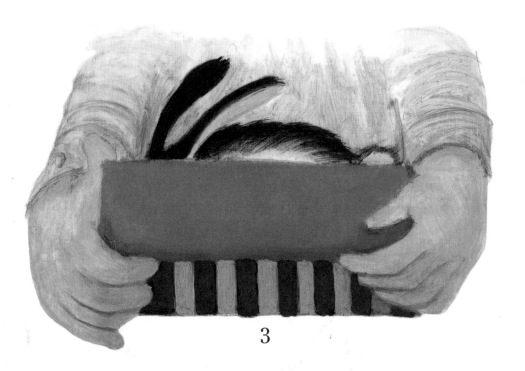

The rabbit had a note tied around its neck. "Take good care of my baby," the note read.

"Who would leave a rabbit at the movies?" Toby asked.

"Especially a scary movie like *Dracula*," said Pete.

"Dracula?" Chester gasped. Of course, no one heard him except me.

"What shall we name him?" Toby asked.

"How about Fluffy?" Mrs. Monroe suggested.

Oh, there she goes again, I thought. Mrs. Monroe was always trying to name some poor pet Fluffy. Chester and I had both been Fluffy for a few terrible days.

"Let's call him Dracula," Toby said.

"That's dumb!" Pete cried.

"Is not!"

"Is so!"

"Now, boys, we'll have to come up with a name both of you can agree on," Mr. Monroe said.

"Okay," the boys said, but they didn't sound too sure.

Mrs. Monroe thought for a moment. "Let's see, we found him in a Dracula movie, and he's a bunny rabbit. . . . How about Bunny-cula. Bunnicula!"

"Not bad," Pete said with a laugh.

"Perfect!" Toby agreed. "Count Bunnicula!"

Crack!

At that very moment there was a clap of thunder and a flash of lightning. The rabbit's eyes glowed red. But no one seemed to notice.

Except Chester and me.

"I wish they had named him Fluffy," Chester said.

CHAPTER 2:

The White Tomato

Not much happened at first. The Monroes made Bunnicula a home out of an old cage. They set it on the table near the window.

Bunnicula slept a lot. In fact, he slept all day. As soon as the sun went down, he would wake up. Then he would hop around a little.

The boys tried to play with him. But he did not fetch. He did not play tug-of-war. He did not chew on old shoes.

"A rabbit is cute but not much fun," I said to myself. I was talking to myself a lot lately, since Chester was not much fun either. Chester had been acting very strangely ever since Bunnicula arrived.

"I have to keep an eye on that rabbit," Chester said.

"Why?" I asked. "He's just a cute little bunny."

"Cute little bunny!" Chester gasped. "He is a danger to this household and everyone in it!"

Now, there's something I should

tell you about Chester. He has a big imagination. I think it comes from reading too many books.

"A danger? How?" I asked.

"I don't know yet," Chester said. "But I am going to find out."

So every night Chester spied on the bunny. He reported back to me in the morning.

"That rabbit has strange markings."

"You mean his spots?" I asked.

"But all together the spots look like a black cape!" Chester hissed.

The next day Chester said, "That rabbit has fangs! I saw them gleaming in the moonlight!"

"So?"

"So rabbits aren't supposed to have fangs. They are supposed to have little rabbit teeth."

One morning Chester had some real news.

"That rabbit got out of his cage last night."

"Don't be silly," I replied. "How could he break through the wire?"

"That's just it! He didn't break through any wire. He got out without breaking anything or opening any doors!"

"And then what did he do?"

"I don't know," Chester said. "But he was doing something in the kitchen."

"Maybe it was Mr. Monroe," I suggested. I knew how Mr. Monroe liked midnight snacks.

"No," Chester said. "It was
Bunnicula."

Just then we heard voices in the kitchen.

"What in the world is this?" Mr. Monroe asked.

"Gee, Dad, it looks like a tomato," Pete said.

"But it's all white," Toby added.

Mrs. Monroe got out a knife and cut the thing in two.

"It's a tomato, all right. But it's all dried out," she said. "There's no juice at all."

Chester dragged me into the living room for a talk. "A white tomato," he said. "Very scary."

"What's so scary about a white tomato?" I asked.

"There were marks on the skin!" Chester cried.

"What kind of marks?"

"Teeth marks."

I felt a chill run up my spine. We both turned to look at Bunnicula. He was sound asleep in his cage. And he was smiling.

Chapter 3:

The Vampire Bunny

The next morning I was awakened by a scream. It was Mrs. Monroe. She was in the kitchen. There were more white vegetables. They were everywhere.

White zucchini.

White carrots.

White beans and white peas.

White lettuce and more white tomatoes.

"What could it mean?" Mrs. Monroe gasped.

"Maybe there is something wrong with our refrigerator," Mr. Monroe said.

"Maybe the vegetables are sick," Pete said.

"It's Bunnicula," Chester told me. "He's a vampire bunny."

"A what?" I asked.

Chester pulled out a book he had been reading.

"This tells you everything you ever wanted to know about vampires," Chester said.

I had never wanted to know
anything about vampires, but I didn't
say so. I listened as Chester went
through the list.

"One, vampires sleep all day. Two, vampires can get through locked doors. Three, vampires bite people on the neck."

I had never seen Bunnicula bite anyone, and I said so.

"Well, Bunnicula bites vegetables," Chester said.

"On the neck?" I asked.

"Vegetables don't have necks." Chester sighed. "Just like dogs don't have brains."

That hurt my feelings. "I think all rabbits bite vegetables." I sniffed.

"Yes, but Bunnicula bites vegetables with his fangs and sucks out all the juices. That's why the vegetables turn white."

I had to admit that the white vegetables were pretty strange. Still, I could not believe that a harmless-looking ball of fluff was really a vampire.

But Chester was sure, and he decided to do something about it.

Chapter 4:

Chester's Smelly Plan

That night I could not sleep. Strange sounds were coming from the kitchen. A strange odor was in the air. I went downstairs to investigate. I found Chester wearing an odd necklace.

"What is that?" I asked.

"Garlic."

"Why do you have it around your neck?"

"Because vampires hate garlic."

"Phew! I can understand why!"

The smell was so strong, I felt sick to my stomach. I looked around.

There was garlic everywhere. On the floor. In the doorways. Around the windows. There was garlic all around Bunnicula's cage.

The poor little guy was hiding under a blanket. I wanted to do the same. I started to go back to Toby's room, but Chester caught me.

"Here, put this on!" he cried.

"No way!" I yelped. I got out of there as fast as I could.

In the morning there were more screams.

Not again, I thought. *What's turned white now?*

It was Chester. He was in the sink, covered in soap.

"Chester, I don't know what got into you last night," Mrs. Monroe was saying. "But I hope this teaches you to stay out of the garlic!"

Chapter 5:

A New Friend

Over the next few days there were no more white vegetables. And Chester was the perfect cat. He purred. He cooed. He cleaned his paws. He rubbed up against everyone's legs. It made me worried. Chester acted that way only when he was planning something.

"What are you up to?" I asked.

Chester did not answer. He had not spoken to me since I had refused to wear the garlic.

So I started hanging out by Bunnicula's cage. Bunnicula didn't speak to me either, but he was a good listener. I was beginning to like the little fellow.

One evening I noticed that my new friend did not look well. It was dark, but he wasn't moving around. His ears drooped. His nose was hot and dry.

I tried to tell the Monroes, but they
did not understand what I was
barking about. So I decided to keep
an eye on the bunny myself.

Late that night I went downstairs.
I found Bunnicula's cage empty. I
found Bunnicula on the floor near
the kitchen. Chester was there, too.
And he had been into the garlic again.

"Chester, what are you doing?"
I cried.

"I am protecting the kitchen from
that monster," he hissed.

Now I understood why Bunnicula
looked sick and why there had been
no white vegetables.

Chester was starving Bunnicula!

"That little bunny never hurt anybody," I said. "What do you care if he drains a few vegetables?"

"He's a vampire!" Chester snarled. "Today, vegetables. Tomorrow . . . the world!"

Chester was getting carried away. I made up my mind to help Bunnicula. I knew it would not be easy. Chester was a hard cat to cross.

CHAPTER 6:

A Helping Paw

The next day I tried to come up with a plan to help Bunnicula. I knew I didn't have much time. Bunnicula was looking pretty droopy.

Around suppertime I started to panic. That's when I stumbled into the dining room. And there it was right in front of me. The answer to my problem.

A big bowl of salad.

"Now, how do I get the bunny to the greens?" I asked myself.

I checked the kitchen. Mrs. Monroe was still working on the rest of dinner. They all sat down to eat.

I checked the window. The sun was setting fast. That meant Bunnicula would be waking up soon.

I checked Chester. He was sound asleep.

I went to Bunnicula's cage and
opened the latch. As gently as I
could, I took the little bunny in my
mouth and carried him to the dining
room.

"Okay," I whispered. "There's your
dinner. Go to it!"

Bunnicula's eyes opened. He
looked at the salad. He looked at me.

"Hurry!" I said, and I gave him a
little push.

I didn't have to push him again. Bunnicula made a mad dash for the salad bowl.

"That's one hungry bunny," I said. I felt very proud of my plan.

But then the door crashed open. Chester had woken up!

"Oh no you don't!" Chester shrieked.

He took a flying leap and almost landed on top of Bunnicula.

The poor bunny did not know what to do. He hopped straight up into the air

and came down right in the salad. Lettuce and tomatoes and carrots and cucumbers went flying. The whole family came running.

"What's going on in here?"
Mrs. Monroe cried. She grabbed
Chester and stared at him. "First it's
garlic and now it's salad? I don't
know what's come over you."
Chester did not even try to move.

CHAPTER 7:

A Happy Ending

The Monroes could not figure out what was going on, but they did see that something was wrong.

"Bunnicula looks sick!" Toby cried.

"Let's take him to the vet," Mr. Monroe said.

"Let's take everybody to the vet," Mrs. Monroe suggested.

"Oh, great," I muttered. Going to the vet is not my favorite thing to do.

We all piled into the car. The vet saw us right away. He said that Bunnicula was suffering from hunger. He gave Bunnicula some carrot juice so the bunny would get his food faster.

The vet said that the reason Chester had been acting so funny was because he was jealous of Bunnicula.

"Jealous?" Chester said. "Of a vampire? What kind of doctor is he?"

When the vet said I was in perfect health and gave me a doggie treat, I told Chester, "A good doctor!"

Now everything is great in the
Monroe household. Bunnicula liked
the juice diet so much, the Monroes
kept him on it. So there have been no
more white vegetables. And Chester
seems to be his old self again—which
is not to say that he is completely
normal. He *is* a cat, after all. And I
like to tease him now and then.

"So, Chester?"

"Yes, Harold?"

"Do you still think Bunnicula is a
vampire bunny?"

"Of course. But he's a modern vampire. He gets his juices from the blender."

"So, um, Chester?"

"Yes, Harold?"

"What are those two funny marks on your neck?"

Chester jumped a very high jump.

"Very funny," he said when he came down.

"Very funny."